Animals Everywhere!

Based on The Railway Series
by the Reverend W Awdry
Illustrated by Richard Courtney

Random House 🏠 New York

Dear Parent:

Congratulations! Your child is taking the first steps on an exciting journey. The destination? Independent reading!

STEP INTO READING® will help your child get there. The program offers five steps to reading success. Each step includes fun stories and colorful art. There are also Step into Reading Sticker Books, Step into Reading Math Readers, Step into Reading Phonics Readers, Step into Reading Write-In Readers, and Step into Reading Phonics Boxed Sets—a complete literacy program with something to interest every child.

Learning to Read, Step by Step!

Ready to Read   Preschool–Kindergarten
• big type and easy words • rhyme and rhythm • picture clues
For children who know the alphabet and are eager to begin reading.

Reading with Help   Preschool–Grade 1
• basic vocabulary • short sentences • simple stories
For children who recognize familiar words and sound out new words with help.

Reading on Your Own   Grades 1–3
• engaging characters • easy-to-follow plots • popular topics
For children who are ready to read on their own.

Reading Paragraphs   Grades 2–3
• challenging vocabulary • short paragraphs • exciting stories
For newly independent readers who read simple sentences with confidence.

Ready for Chapters   Grades 2–4
• chapters • longer paragraphs • full-color art
For children who want to take the plunge into chapter books but still like colorful pictures.

STEP INTO READING® is designed to give every child a successful reading experience. The grade levels are only guides. Children can progress through the steps at their own speed, developing confidence in their reading, no matter what their grade.

Remember, a lifetime love of reading starts with a single step!

Thomas the Tank Engine & Friends™

CREATED BY BRITT ALLCROFT

Based on The Railway Series by The Reverend W Awdry.
© 2011 Gullane (Thomas) LLC.
Thomas the Tank Engine & Friends and Thomas & Friends are trademarks of
Gullane (Thomas) Limited.
HIT and the HIT Entertainment logo are trademarks of HIT Entertainment Limited.

HIT entertainment

All rights reserved. Published in the United States by Random House Children's Books,
a division of Random House, Inc., 1745 Broadway, New York, NY 10019, and in Canada by
Random House of Canada Limited, Toronto.

Step into Reading, Random House, and the Random House colophon are registered
trademarks of Random House, Inc.

Visit us on the Web!
StepIntoReading.com
www.randomhouse.com/kids
www.thomasandfriends.com

Educators and librarians, for a variety of teaching tools, visit us at
www.randomhouse.com/teachers

ISBN: 978-0-375-86812-2 (trade pbk.) — ISBN: 978-0-375-96827-3 (lib. bdg.)

Printed in the United States of America
10 9 8 7 6 5 4 3 2 1

The circus is
coming to town!
Thomas is excited.

There is a
big striped tent.
There is
cotton candy.

And there are
lots and lots
of animals.

One monkey
even plays music!

Thomas wants
to be part of the circus.
"Engines cannot
join the circus,"
says James.

A girl drops
her ice cream.
A man from the
circus helps her.

The monkey
takes the man's
keys.

The monkey

unlocks

the circus cars!

The animals climb out.

The children
go into the tent.

14

They clap.
They cheer.
But the show
does not begin.

A clown runs out
of the tent.
He is upset.
The animals
are missing!

Thomas does not want
the children
to miss the circus.

"Peep! Peep!
I will find them!"
says Thomas.

The ticket man
connects Thomas
to the circus cars.

Clickety-clack!

Clickety-clack!

Thomas puffs

down the track.

Animals are
everywhere!
Thomas finds a lion.
He is leaping
over a lawn chair.

Thomas finds

an elephant.

She is bouncing a ball.

Thomas finds a bear.
He is riding
a boy's bike.

Thomas finds two seals.

They are splashing

in the town pool.

Where is the monkey?

Thomas looks
and looks.
Finally,
Thomas finds
the monkey.

He is juggling dishes.

Crash! Clang!

Smash! Bang!

Clickety-clack!
Clickety-clack!
Thomas drives
the animals back.

"Thank you,"
says the ticket man.
"You saved
the circus!"

The monkey gives
Thomas his silly hat.
The clown gives
Thomas a red nose.

"I was wrong,"
says James.
"You are
a circus engine!"